About the Author

Anna Kapungu is a poet, children's book writer and singer/songwriter. She has a Bachelor of Arts honours degree in Hospitality Management from the University of South Bank, London, UK. She is a citizen of Canada, who emigrated to the United Kingdom, and now lives in Buckinghamshire.

Dedication

This book is dedicated to Phoenix.

Anna Kapungu

WATER FALLING
BETWEEN WORDS

AUSTIN MACAULEY
PUBLISHERS LTD.

A CIP catalogue record for this title is available from the British Library.

ISBN 9781786127112 (Paperback)
ISBN 9781786127129 (Hardback)
ISBN 9781786127136 (eBook)
www.austinmacauley.com

First Published (2017)
Austin Macauley Publishers Ltd.
25 Canada Square
Canary Wharf
London
E14 5LQ

Acknowledgments

My family for their continued support, the Mhangwas my adopted parents and Martyn Shaw.

POEMS ON NATURE

POEMS ON LIFE IN SOCIETY

POEMS ON LIFE

PARADISE

Sunlit sky so blue, face to the sun
Yellow dress, yellow roses, sand between my toes
Blue ocean meets blue sky, there is a horizon
Whites beaches, high cliffs, no earthquakes
My abode, I desire
Easy life, easy time and everything new

White rippling tides
Waves against the cliff
Sleep comes easy, sounds like Chinese charms on my
doorstep
Seagulls glide through white moonlight
Peace all around and I breathe easy

Searchlight on the seawater, star light in the dark sky
Rhythm of the ocean and echoes of the depth
Twilight cold and singing nightingales
Close my eyes and it feels like home.

PHOENIX

My love is complete
Since with you I met
Your tiny hands and feet
My love and heart beat

This is more than fate
It was destiny, my heart
You are a work of art
My shining star, my starlight

To love, with all my might
Kisses, caresses, drops of water sweet
Like summer heat, my heart melts
What is this love, I have never felt

My dreams, and plans and everything wrought
This love, never I thought
Like an oasis in the desert
Magical like sunlight and sunset

Our lives with you are blessed
My every day, my delight
The light under the moonlight
I am lost without.

EPWORTH

Freedom unbridled, peace without understanding
Love at first sight, beautiful with no faults
Unimaginable, my roots, home and all its comforts
My love in this land I did find
Beauty within a life I cannot understand
Luxury without ego, life as it was meant to be
Like an oasis in the desert
I found my corner of the world
Water like blue, yellow like the sun
I am empty without, forever my paradise.

BEHIND THE FACE

Behind the glasses, the hunchback and 50's dresses
Under the calm, cool and concerned look
Inside the mind of the tired face, Miss Prissy and neat clothes
The story is yet to unfold.

Behind the dishevelled, tired and hurried look
Under the small, bony and fragile interior
Inside the mind of the overweight, aggressive and forceful character
The picture tells the story.

Behind the handsome, quiet, familiar face
Inside the mind of the dancer at the party
Under the old, friendly and frail character of the priest
The story has unfolded.

Behind the loud, dirty beggar seated at the corner
Inside the mind of the man with the hundred-dollar bill
Under the skin of the withdrawn, quiet neighbour
There the river runs deep.

BREAK OF DAWN

Ends just as it is written, today breaks the dawn
Memories I have hidden, yesterday's toils and sorrow
Tomorrow, no-one can foretell
But today, cumulus clouds, the rainfall I await

Today, I am quiet, fragile and weak within,
The end of a relationship's foreseen and yesterday's
remorseless anger and turmoil
Tomorrow, no-one can foretell
But today, cumulus clouds, the rainfall I await

Falsely, silently, today the hours decay slowly
Helpless confinement, disappointments, my frustrations
that was yesterday
Tomorrow, no-one can foretell
But today, cumulus clouds, the rainfall I await

The sunset, indifferent today, like any other, peace
within
Tears, my heart is hardened, yesterday's war and
bitterness
Tomorrow, no-one can foretell
But today, cumulus clouds, the rainfall I awaits.

THE FLOW OF MY TEARS

Home and everything that's new
Lift my hands, breathe in the fresh air
My mind free and its new beginnings
No worries, life has just begun
Close to tears, freedom never felt
Close to exhaustion, long road to freedom
My knees buckling, finally I am free
The spirit accepts pleasure, I'm awake
Silence to find myself
Peace within
Close my eyes and let my mind rest
Nothing to do and everything to feel
Where have I been?

RISE OF THE PHOENIX

Closest to the light
Victory in sight
Release darkness
Acceptance of new beginnings
Life redirecting itself
The heart's resolve
At test of character
All things matter
The rise of the phoenix
Release fear
Release tears
There is silence in the heart
At the end of the tunnel, light
There resides wisdom
The answer, a revelation.

LILY

A red rose in the midst of the winter storm
A well in the heat of the desert sun
The rock in the midst of the blue ocean
Sunshine during a rainstorm
The eye of the hurricane
That is who you are to me.

THE ACTOR

Play a role on the stage called life
The childlike woman I hide
The artistic hunger for expression
The world to open its doors to my light

Play a role on stage called life
Fear in trust and time
Time, my adversary, each second an addition
Additions which lessen my time for expression

Play a role on the stage called life
The molten heat of anger that resides within
Cries out to me, the tormented soul
Hate and disdain of self who I have become
Words of wisdom but I am speechless

Play a role on the stage called life
Through my eyes who I am
Decays inside the human, I love
Emotions unable to utter and display

Play a role on the stage called life
Fear who I am, the person inside
A well of miseries, a forest of mysteries
Imperfect and human all I am

THE ROCK IN THE MIDDLE OF THE OCEAN

All seasons you brave the elements alone
Storms of life attack but still you stand

Wave after wave, at sunrise the core is unmoved
Majesty and grace, your height not lessened, aspect
viewed from a far

Dark and grey as the winter, but inside the colour of
sunlight
Thunderstorms and lightning chip away,

Polishes the outside that is the diamond in you
Strength and power in silence

Like yellow roses in the sun, you are still standing
The rock in the middle of the ocean.

I AM WOMAN

Just because I am small
I have the strength of a thousand
Travelled all around the world
Speak so many different languages
Courted princes and paupers

Read psychology, biology and geography
Accent distinct very Americana
Not a commoner but not royalty
A heart that is full of love

Creativity is where it resides
Poetry in motion, a body build to last
Laugh like water, sing like rain
Dreams of life, that's what I will become.

THE FUNERAL

The week ended as it was not envisioned
Daddy in a coffin, a tuxedo and bottle of rum
The secret was finally out
Teacups and sandwiches down
Mouths agape, horror and disbelief
Silence and numbness, minds and their own thoughts
This was a story for the telling
His existence not a mirror of his image
Still water does run deep
How was his memory going to live up to this?

SALT OF THE EARTH

Just like its name comes from the ground
Just like water one cannot live without
Your aura, person that you are, we need
Your essence, your being, the person of wonder that's
salt
Grounded, humble, you are the salt of the earth

The taste you know by now
It changeth not unless you desire it to
Like you, the person you know
So aware of you, your charm, your charisma
Grounded, humble, you are salt of the earth

White as snow, it remains the same
Unassuming, each day is a day you are in need of it
You are an oasis to sit and let me be grounded
Swallow up your knowledge, I am full of it
You are the home that is my place, peace in time
Grounded humble, you are the salt of the earth

One never asks or begs of it
At the beginning, middle and end of the day
Look for you in my haze and daze that is this life
Like a light, everything makes sense
Just like you, you never ask for more
No one can compare
Grounded, humble you are the salt of earth.

LIFE

Every day is life
Perspective with the full picture
Directed sunlight to sundown
The hour dictates the day
Plans for the future
Maturity, a reality of experience
Pictured
Life is everyday.

POEMS ON LOVE

THE UNION

My love is true, carries no fault
Loyalty with strength bears no wrongs
The state of this love, this journey's obstacles, does not change it
The turmoil in its path, strengthens the union
Immeasurable in length, width and height, this is love immense
Its direction it alters not
Loyalty without doubt
If I am wrong, may love be the fault.

POSSESSION

Should I possess you, your being overwhelms
Beauty understated I disdain myself
Love too pure, your life I cannot hide
I give you up, freedom you deserve
To the world, I give, a true Gift of God
Better than me, a man you deserve
If you should remain, if that is your wish and desire
My worth to you is love all encompassing
Live as I am, joyful of your presence in my life
Return to me, if love is still in your heart.

DEEPER THAN THE CORE

Love is like a woman
Acceptance with no rejection
Thick as molasses it is full circle
Pure as the heart no bitterness it carries
Honesty without doubt, no sorrow in the horizon
Loyalty in anger, emotions the heart remain
A game no one wins one plays for a lifetime
A test of character, in pleasure or regret
Long suffering and patience in all things
Loves the wounded heart who remains in any circumstance
Mysterious soul, nymph, deeper into its core
The careful child who promised forever
It is blind, deaf with loyalty
Never loses hope, always accepts, always waits with open arms
Love is like a child: falls in love innocently
Never changing, constant as the seasons.

SWEET RAPTURE

Love undisturbed that was you and me
Sweet rapture morning after
A true man to me was your being
The future that was you and me

Laugh early in the morning
Lunch dates in the afternoon
Used to be picture perfect harmony
Made love under the moon

In every way torn apart by circumstance
Everyday breaking down, was this love?
Cherish, something got in the way
What happened to this love?

Used to smile at the sound of your voice in my ear
Sweet nothings early in the morning
Used to smile at mystery of love growing
Sweet days, anticipation of you.

SUMMERLILY

Nights never seemed so long
While you lie naked next to me
My spirit longs to touch the woman in you
My heart at present belongs to another
Love with you is like yellow roses in autumn
I long for love unconditional
Happiness unsurmountable
Joy and sentience I do not have.
Your big smile, I carry in me always
The baby voice, where did you come from?
Hazel brown eyes, intense, you are salt of the earth
When you laugh, it's like water and pearls
Fresh air on your face
Beauty, I am without.

LOVE

Love is a careless child
A cruel affliction of the mind
Innocent enough to think it will find itself
No control of its direction or destination
Irrational in its will and at worst uncontrollable
Pure feeling understandable an energy that flows
An inner torment to one's despair
Changeth not, diminishes not
Evolves, everlasting and always in you
It's a foundation, a place called home.

LOVE REMAINS

Darling, if you should ever change, I will never love again
If you should cry, then I am not a man
If you should be sad, then my love fails
If you should be displeased, I will try again

If you should fear, know my love is secure
If you should doubt, know my love remains
If you should be impatient, time and love it did build
If you should ever tire, then know my love is strong
If you are wise, it brings joy to my soul
If you smile, then know all is well
If you should laugh, it is the fruit of our love
If you should love me, then love is complete.

RAINE

Tiny hands and tiny feet
Light brown eyes and golden hair
Finally, you arrived
Blessed to have you in my life

Milky breath and toothless grins
Your sighs and cries
I am alive
Blessed to have you in my life

Precious to this life
Your journey has just begun
That's all I ever wanted
Blessed to have you in my life

Blank page to fill
Your life's journey and experiences
Instructions I will provide
Blessed to have you in my life

Your first date and graduation
You will be a man
Life awaits your growth
Blessed to have you in my life.

LOVE AT FIRST SIGHT

Love at first sight
Dimples on your face
Soft spoken words I can barely hear
Smile at me as if I was your last
Understood me the day we met
Sleep don't come easy
Hazy days filled with you
Sigh at the woman you are
Strong willed, motivated and goodness in your heart
Laughter and pain, a love I never had
You are poetry in motion
Something like magic in my life
You personify elegance and grace
I never envisioned
Smart and sophisticated know things about the world
Wisdom on your lips
May the best of life
Be everything that was given to you.

IMPOSSIBLE

What am I looking for?
Quite contrary
Love without turmoil or instability
Inner peace and self-respect or tyranny
Never dull the senses or sanity
Without grief or tears, darkness and despair
Is it a sin to love?

HUMAN STANDARDS

My love is immense
Rare by definition
Begotten from cruelty
Impossible by human standards

My love is magnanimous
Pure in its form
Begotten from despair
Impossible by human standards

My love is glorious
Golden as the morning sunlight
Begotten from sorrow
Impossible by human standards

My love is endless
Beautiful in its nature
Begotten from torment
Impossible by human standards.

MY LIFE IN YOUR HANDS

Blue as the cloudless sky, those are your eyes
Dark and flowing against the moonlight, that is your hair
Full as the river after the rain, those are your lips
Meandering like the Nile, that is your essence
Beauty, that's mine to behold.

AUTUMN-ROSE

Autumn-rose
You are the rose in my vision that's time
Your smile I live for each day
Your childlike spirit we all embrace
You are beauty personified
True and gifted all in one
My soul longs to touch you
My heart hurts with everything you do
Society that is aloof and no one to say I love you
Perfect in your silence
You are the star in my life
The strongest woman walking this planet
Humble to a fault where have you been all my life?
No one understands
You are the red rose on a dark autumn morning.

POEMS ON NATURE

EARTH

The excellence that is oblivious and magnificent
Indescribable, the energy of our lives
Radiation survival is our dependency
The artist that is the one, creator of the universe
A wonder to humanity

Like a rainbow beauty that is
A sight to behold, water like blue
A volcanic mass, untameable it has a rhythm
Rhythm, universe, all it controls

Without, humanity uninhabitable
Lack of vision, no balance
Humanity encircles with each passing day
The ticking clock that marks each day within us

Colour of light that is
Constant warmth is like the rays of the sun
Warmth, that fills humanity
Nourishes and grows us, that is the earth.

HOME

Chart a course through and beyond
Millions of stars riding the Milky Way
Pinks, silvers, yellows this is home
Shooting stars, asteroids, rocks and dust
Travelling 64000 miles per hour
Mercury, Venus, Mars our neighbours
Black clouds, meteors, dark energy of flowing electricity
Expressions and wind's formulation
Moving towards a collision course, Andromeda
Moon, stars and the sun
That's our stability
Our universe ever changing… still.

SUNSET

Half-sun and the quiet lake
Red chested robins fly easterly
Moonlight fills the sky
Orange glow, the sun is descending

Cool breeze, spring night darkness is near
Silver light shining stars over yonder
Light showers, sleep comes easy
Wild life by nature's bank's they drink

Night is falling, the scents of flora
Crickets creaking, shadows all around
The day is gone, silence
Daybreak, it's sunrise again.

NOVEMBER

The clouds are low dark and grey
Black is the sky
The occasional single bird flying in an easterly or westerly
The quiet cold winter around the bay
No sunshine to lift my mood today

The wind, cold, brisk, as the trees sway
The ground frozen, covered with ice and fallen leaves today
Not even the rise of the tide, the gaze of the moon and still of the sky
Reflects the stillness within me, why?

The trees are bare, frozen and it is a November day
The landscape a mesh of yellows, greens and reds, winter is on its way
The single bark of the neighbour's dog breaks the silence today
From the quiet, still night dawn is breaking

It's a dreary winter's morning
Nature unfolds its beauty
The stream trickles to the Bay of Falling
Nature is quiet, peaceful and distant, winter is here to stay.

FROZEN WINTER

Beauty of the earth and it's white as snow
Rays of the sun, yellow its daybreak
Clear blue sky, ice cold air
Frozen ground, migrating swans
Trickle of the water down the stream
Frozen bare trees in the icy cold lake
Cold, easterly winds, autumn leaves in the air
Dark, cumulus clouds, thunderstorms and lightning
Hailstones on my window pane, snow on my rooftop
Winter is here to stay.

LOST

Dark, stormy Monday morning
Vast snow on the ground, winds blowing
Temperature -44 degrees with hailstones
The air is icy, the breath is warm
My fingers are frozen
The crunch of the snow
The mind loses heat
What is the street again?
Blank stare my vision blurred
The houses seem to move
What street is it again?
No stranger in sight, I must get inside
The cutting wind is cruel, my face is frozen
My steps are little, time it takes to get home
I thought this was the street
I must have come down the wrong way
My breath laboured, weakness in my limbs
Feeling dazed, I stagger
I thought I saw a house
My voice is slight, hoarse, I can hardly shout
Confused, my heart beats slowly
On my knees, I need help.

LOUISIANA

Alligators and standing waters
Swamps, mosquitoes, lakes with something to hide
Cajun food and French pâtés, patois
Spiced tripe and okra
Creole food, nights and Jazz in the blue room
Bed and breakfast, pink rooms and tilted accents
Sharp striped clothes, multicultural and I think I'm home
Trams and tree lined roads
Colonial white houses, rich folks with Rolls Royces
Time and leisure
Beauty at the bayou
Tales of Huckleberry Finn and Tom Sawyer
Heat all year, think I might stay here forever.

WINTER'S MORNING

Silence in the house
Crackle of the fireplace
The dark, rainy Monday morning
Howling winds and leaves in the air
Dark stratus clouds and my mood is grey

Silently, in the crib the baby sleeping
The smell of fresh baked bread in the kitchen
Clink of Chinese charms on the doorstep
In the hallway the chimes of my grandfather's clock

The shuffle of the Chow Chow in the bedroom playing
Warmth I feel against the cold outside
Soft sounds of the voice on the television screen
The tea in my body keeping me warm
It's a winter's Monday morning, outside a place I do not
want to be.

FARGO

Snow covered, hard ground, ice storm that lasts for days
Temperature -44 and blustery cold North Arctic winds,
Brown, sparse tundra grass and small brick cottages in
the distance
Chimney smokes and orange light filled windows
Beef stew and smells of baked potatoes
Truckers driving by to the oil in the west
White, snowy landscape as far as the eye can see
High mountains of snow and streams of ice
Down to the Mississippi it melts
The sounds of the axe as the farmer chops the wood
Dark cirro stratus clouds and silence all around.

RAINBOW

Storm ceases, sunlight on the day
Colour in the sky, once in a blue moon
Range of vitality, colours of the earth
Mirrors his image, spirit in our lives
Beautiful in itself, human nature still exists
Glorious its presence, beauty like magnificence

JULY DAY

Hot, summer morning
The sun is ascending

Misty dew on the ground
Beetles in the meadows abound

White, cumulus clouds and blue sky
Seagulls at the bay

Strong, warm winds blowing
The earth is shifting

Gentle currents, the shore it reaches
Seashells and pearls on the sandy beaches

Heat rises, warmth in the air and sky
This is a July day.

DECEMBER SUN

Sunlight and all things green
December sun, no snow in sight
Early morning light and dark, late nights
Fields of crops and fruits everywhere
Little cottages amongst beautiful landscapes
Blue rivers and nature by the koppies
Wild horses run free and mountain goats everywhere
February blue blossoms and honey drops
Children play in fields of buttercups
Beautiful sunsets and long peaceful nights
Ah, to be home again.

KARIBA

Sunrise at four, cruises on the lake
Sun sizzles, heat waves on the ground
Crickets in the air, it's hot and humid
Perspiration like water
Thirst like the desert
It's hard to cool down
Stillness in the lake
Danger in the air
Cries of vultures, scavengers for life
Movements in the forests, life exists everywhere
No walks in the midday sun
Classical music on the radio
Tea and scones for afternoon tea
Nature at the reservoir at sunset
Nights under the moonlight.

SOLAR SYSTEM

Gravitational pull, orbit singular
The pull of the solar system, light's radiation
Elements and minerals, dark matter all around
Planets the colour of rainbows, moving points of light
Moon the stabilizer, planet paths it maintains
Seasons and years, earth rotation reliance.

POEMS ON LIFE IN SOCIETY

THIS PART OF TOWN

Drug dealers on the doorsteps
Bullets in the hallway
Strange smells in the corridor
The neighbour's wife screaming at the children
Trash bins on the stairways
No one answers the calls for help
The hospital shut down for two years
Police shoot to kill
Teenage moms on welfare
Children in poverty who live on government stamps
Young men with no jobs all year
Liquor store around the corner and bullets for sale
No nursing homes in this part of town.

OUT OF ORDER

Depressed mind, happy exterior
Trying to control this life, clutter everywhere
Smiling faces, cruelty in the heart
Hoarders in the home, extroverts to society
Communication none, cheerful social family
Materialistic, loyalty to no-one
Happy children, lacking in foundation
Live day by day, a house for sleeping
Need for social authority
The absence of parental guidance
Out of order, chaos that exists.

DISILLUSIONED

Young to the ways of life I'm disillusioned
Snakes in my existence I was corrupted

Hungry for a fresh start and fast money
It should have been a must, success and honesty

My way of life redirected into shame
My creativity, intelligence, I did maim

In full stupidity I was confirmed
At every station my spirit was damned

Thoughtless and irrational understanding
The love of a man I thought I was maintaining

Numb within the lure of money, my calling
Tears of pain, my joy I was abandoning

My fate complete, I was living with the damned
Trembling with fear, I weep for the days I possessed

SOLITUDE

Forgotten in love
Not of my choosing
A place of hurt
I am alone
Peace within me
Defence against the world
Treated me unkindly
Nothing too good to feel or be
A place of reflection
Brought peace and love unto this spirit
Resist this place I know
I do not want to be alone.

A FACE IN THE CROWD

A face in the crowd
I thought you were familiar
Uncomfortable you
I know how you tilt your head
The way you walk
In the crowd that is the face of you

A face in the crowd
I peer so you do not perceive
Unmistakeable you
You stick out even when you hide
The way your hand holds your suitcase
In the crowd that's the face of you

A face in the crowd
I bet you cannot reminisce
Uncanny is it not?
You smile as if you have no worries
The light of your eyes, that is you
In the crowd that is the face of you

A face in the crowd
I bet you did not deem we would meet in a place like this
So close yet so far away
Unimaginable is it not?
Crowd so loud, I can barely hear my breathing
In the crowd that is the face of you.

A LIFE I DON'T HAVE

Something about being cold and alone
Negativity heavy without
Pain in me cries for help
The light in the window
A life I do not have

Something about being alone in the dark
Pain people passing me by in the street
The need for love
Everything that is human
A life I do not have

Something about aloneness that is nothing
Empty cannot wait for tomorrow
Darkness that is desperation
No home to call my own
A life I do not have.

BROKEN GLASS

Love had commenced and ceased that was the awareness
Hollow emptiness, wounded in a daze of love that was
the sense
Unworthy in love a self-realization
Affection withdrawal is inner desperation

Released fondness became insecurity of love
Deserted love through fears within
Withdrawal of self-expression and love barricaded
My heart a shelter of new love, will it without a thought

Without a home you know
Age in society, that is rejection
Thoughts array without silence
Inability to conquer love, self-defeat

Mirror image distorted degradation of self
Waning of self-confidence is loneliness complete
Broken glass of raw emotions
Hate released and sanity returned.

CRY

Space, my mind on blank
Alone comfort that is avoidance
In every moment pain exists
Back of my eyes, my tears reside

Emotions I try to figure out
Sound of the stream and emptiness
It should be pain but numbness exists
Utter my pain, my helplessness

Shadow of the sun, defines my time
Sleepless, endless nights
Moments, I cannot take back or reverse
Silence, peace it brings

Darkness, my only comfort
My whole being on empty
Sound of the clock
The seconds…I cry.

AFFLICTED

My poverty, my disgrace, my solitude
Turmoil and sorrow, I am without
Not the world can comprehend my destitution
Curse the day I was afflicted
Long for relief to uplift my mood

In destitution I am alone
Laughter in sorrow, laughter that's emptiness
The mirror image of me, a broken glass
Tears that no-one can share

Without love or desire, I detest myself
The want of what I do not possess
Desire, I am lonely as the nights
Under the moonlight.

THE LIGHT WITHIN

Does my humbleness offend you?
Seem more like weakness than who I am?

Does my smile offend you?
Seem like men will lust after me, which I detest?

Does my walk offend you?
It did not come from my womb, it was the gift of God

Does my body offend you?
It is the temple built to last

Does my face offend you?
It is just me striving to make it in this world

Do my hands offend you?
Given to me to work for this life

Does my presence offend you?
So unaware it is the light within.

HATE

Cruelty without humanity
Discriminate is hate's irresponsibility
Feelings without reality
Understandable even to one, no-one knows

The spirit in one absent and obsolete
The spirit of strength and power overcomes
The self that rejects regret
Superiority without self-reins

The invasion of defenceless humanity
Your intention I am aware
Destruction of the mind and body
Unimaginable now I am aware.

THIS TIME

It is a time like this
When nature seems so fragile
Nothing is certain
Instability is common
Tears fill my eyes
Society unforgiving
Love does not live here
Search for home and all its comforts
Paradise, a place I can breathe
A friendly face in the crowd
Someone I can lean on and trust
Love that is certain and true
Have to find my way home.

CRISIS

Migrants on the move
People dying at sea
Planes crash every other week
Gunmen shoot to kill
Instability and uncertainty abound
Corruption, fraud, that's the times we do know
Prayers every day to change and comfort the souls
Bad news is the one that sells
The changing weather, have we noticed
Dark and gloomy is our existence
Populate the earth, the world is spinning
Diseases and death we are all at risk
Nothing matters more than the fragility that is us
Water rising swept by the tides.

HOME

Outside in the dark where life has no meaning
Outside in the dark time is stark
Outside in the dark there is a desperate child within me
Outside in the cold where you pass me by
Outside in the dark where your eyes meet mine
Outside in the cold no-one is coming for me
Outside in the dark where all the cries of pain are mine
Outside in the cold my mood is heavy and dark as the sky
Outside in the dark my existence has no beginning and no joy.

POEMS OF LOST LOVE

WATER UNDER THE BRIDGE

My emotions the water washed away
The hurt in me, like the dry, yellow earth
The fight in me for you, was the turbulence
Always rushing to believe love was waiting for me

Sparks of love, I was like the steam, heat in the water
Love was at its maximum, fed by others, rain from
above, the stream was full
Love in full bloom, contentment and joy from its banks,
nature drunk
Giving love to its most that was my being, fruit that was
true

It all felt apart like lightning and thunderstorm
The love that fed us we fought, just like the rain fed the
stream
Into the sea, the water drained
Through the door, you walked away with my spirit and
being
My broken heart like cracks on the ground cry out

I wait for the spring rain
The ground it will feed
Full again the stream will be and love will reside in me
Home, love would have found

Beautiful like the spirit that was us
As of now
Too much water under the bridge

JEWEL

You look at me with pity
My love, gone to another
Precious you are still
Forgiveness, I cannot fathom
Fury and wrath, I have become
Forgive you, no I cannot
Maybe still in love
Your smile, your walk, all I admire
Your childish ways
I cry with laughter
Wisdom lives on your tongue
Vision of the future, it was always you
In these years, I have become a man
A sight you do not believe
I am without the jewel of my life
Love has no greater meaning than this
You personify grace and dignity in all this weakness
Trust and believe, your light is larger than you envision
Love is always around.

OBJECTS IN MY VISION

Blank stare at the countryside through my window
Emptiness in me, the bleak dark house
Everything seems so loud, it drowns the pain

Blank stare at the page, the words lift to meet the tears in
my eyes
Emptiness in me. water droplets in the bathroom
Everything around makes no sense, I can't breathe

Blank stare at the radio loud without a sound
Emptiness in me, wish I could turn back the hands of
time
Everything around has slowed to motionless, objects in
my vision

Blank stare at the door, no-one opens
Emptiness in me, my heart pulled out, love exists no
more
Everything around is still, I can barely feel.

BLINDED

Love not in your mind
The human in me,
Temporary is the need
You miss the obvious,
In your need you are blinded
I am more human than you know

When you look at me it's not what you see
It's a lasting love that I require
What is it that you look for?
You miss so much in your urgency
Always empty that's what you leave
I am more human than you know

No emotions, no conversations
Left without acknowledgement
I'm trying to find myself
You are not the picture that I needed
You left
The human in me, still hurts.

''

GEOMETRY OF CHANCE

Latitudes crossing at meeting point
Two different worlds, words unspoken
Envisioned the future, not this hour
Thoughtless actions, the present disturbed
A sense of innocence, acceptance to a world unknown
A sense of wonder, tilted life's axis
Lateral journey east to settlement, happiness sought not found
Geometry of chance, I should meet you at this juncture.

GOODBYE

In this moment, what do I feel?
Dry eyed goodbye with no tears
Dare I turn to look back?
Goodbye, words I cannot express

In this moment, what do I feel?
Gone are the intense moments, days and years
To utter those words still unable,
What happened to us?
Goodbye, words I cannot express

In this moment, what do I feel?
A temporary relief, slumber, silence and tears
Days of pain and anguish are what follows
Do I realise, who I was with you?
Goodbye, words I cannot express

In this moment, what do I feel?
How do I become me, the best of me? I see
Nothing to say, feelings supreme
Regroup time to find me
Goodbye words I cannot express

In this moment, what do I feel?
I hang my head and walked away the tears
Was it beautiful, what we had?
May this life mean more today than yesterday
That is my goodbye.

MISDIRECTED

Been excluded, disillusioned, misdirected by love
Been bludgeoned, hated, left behind by love
Love became restricted, abusive and cursed
Love became complicated, disconnected and ingenious

To love, beautiful, my heart was open
Unimaginable, unexplainable and magical,
Exciting it encapsulated my life,
Nurturing, supportive and holding me up, that was love

It's a need unbeknownst to many,
It's a sorrowful cry not known by many,
It's a laugh as beautiful as water,
It's a closeness I never will imagine, that was the love

When I see it again, I will know, that this is love
When it touches me, I will experience love
When it finds me, my heart will be open to love
When its stays, my existence will be fulfilled by love.
But love when will you find me?

WINTER

My unmade bed
The ache in my head
Tears in my eyes reside
Only a day has gone by
Raw emotions, pain still remains
Winter, on my mind

9 o'clock chimes the clock on the wall
Downstairs, the telephone echoes in the hallway
The kettle whistles in the empty house
Only a day has gone by
Raw emotions, pain still remains
Winter, on my mind

Classical music fills the room
Untouched breakfast on my bed
Telephone conversations, none
Only a day has gone by
Raw emotions, pain still remains
Winter, on my mind.

ALONE

A day has gone
Where is my love?
A sense of wonder
Something like emptiness

I'm alone, got that feeling
The same, life just does not seem
A sense of why
Something like helplessness

Where did you go my love?
Good enough, I just was not
Pain still remains
Alone I feel...still
A sense of why
Something like emptiness

Your love you barricaded
Withdrawal of affection, that was you
Fighting for you always, raw emotions
Starting over, what a thought
A sense of wonder
Something like helplessness

Battered, dragged on the ground
That was my love
Who I was you did not accept

Pure love, never embraced
A sense of emptiness and peacefulness
Something like a new day.

WATER FALLING BETWEEN WORDS

Full of wild life, this river was in bloom
Full of expectancy, young love
To the sea the stream trickles
Held up by others, love was at its maximum
Beautiful, crystal clear water for nature
Awareness of us, love was realised
In silence, the energy between us lost
Like the Victoria Falls, water into the depths
They penetrate my heart, your words
Boiling heat scorches the earth
Anger in me, words I cannot express
On the edge of extinction this love, I see
White heat, water rushing to the edge
Dark, hollow emptiness the water into the gorge
The awareness of released fondness, love had ceased
A hundred meters to the bottom, steam in the gorge.

EMPTY WARDROBE

Empty wardrobe and socks on the floor
No note or call to say goodbye
My knees buckle, I can hardly breathe
Tears in my eyes, trust I should have never had
Too much pain, love lost in the fights
Love for another gentle as an angel for you
Cry at stupidity, love I should have kept
You walked into my life and goodness left me
Blessed you have love, ours was not meant
Rage and anger everyday life stood still
Took the joy out of this life
Days of torment we should have left
Blinded by hate
Reality not real, living without vision
I can live without the games, this story I want to live
I let love go and let real love find me.

THE LOVE I NEEDED

Sleepless nights, nights of misery
Misery without you
You, the one I thought I knew
Knew my life was better than this
This circle of pain where you do not exist
Exist in a time I cannot imagine
Imagine my world four years gone
Years gone I cannot reverse
Reverse my thoughts, actions and love I needed
What I needed the most did not need me
Me, the one full of love for you
Love no-one can comprehend
Comprehend this circumstance
Circumstance without providence

POEMS ON WAR AND SOLDIERS

BLOOD IN THE BOGS

Turbulence in the sea, rippling lakes and the river overflow
Ships ashore and bombs in the air
Cracks of rifles, shouts of charge
Invasion of the country
Flowing blood and dying men
Mountainous ridged landscape
Billowing dark smoke
Blood in the bogs
Boots in the mud and flags on the banks
Evergreens once, serenity that was the picture
Children dying, buildings crumbling
Cloudy moon, tears from the sky
Trumpets blowing and death in the air.

CRY FOR HOME

Something about the cold, dark night that's not me
Something about the light that's home to me
Something about the need for familiarity that I do not
have
Something about the light in the window

A wonder about the desperate human I cannot convey
Something in my eyes that cries for home
A helplessness in the way I look at you
Something about the light in the window

Something about the darkness, outside of the warmth
Something about the child that needs a home, in me
Something about the hurt in me that cries for help
Something about the light in the window

A wonder about the human inside the light
Something about the longing for home in me
A helplessness in the lack of shelter
Something about the light in the window.

SILENCE

Peace at last
No more worries, troubles and toils
Gently to the sky lifts the spirit
Joy, bliss all at once, freedom no more restrictions

Assess your days forgive and let go
Face the future that is to come
Your purpose, your place in time you should know
This is glorious second chance, so go

Learn from the past
Freedom allow yourself to feel
Peace at last
Laugh without a care just free to feel

Joy abundant is this the maker
That's the beauty of a second chance
Second chance this is forever
The heart is quiet, no more strife you face
Peace at last.

SOLARIS

Strange as a character in space
Strange as a place I have seen
Unimaginable
State of being altered
Communication flawed
Fear absolute
Actions without thought
Citizens in need of assistance
A spirit overpowers
Fear overpowers.

GATES OF LIFE

When the gate of life arrives
My childhood and days pass me by
When familiar souls and presence I do feel
Light and peace I see

Anxious in myself this is my journey to start
I am humbled and sad within
Judgement I desire but not welcome
Strange a place I see my beginning?

No pain I feel it must be home
Am I alive or alone?
My life far away, it was all meaningless
Life at the moment weighs with meaning

That was the journey
Happiness, sadness, grief and self-torment
My life separated, seems so far away
What do I have to show?

THE PLACE I KNEW

Tried to walk back to the place I knew
The self I knew that others saw
Out of their lives I disappeared
Questions of my minds stagnation.

Tried to walk back to a place I knew
The dreams I never had
The family I never knew
Understanding I always had
Loneliness I loved, my comfort, my bliss

Tried to walk back to a place I knew
Where I was innocent
Life was free, unrestricted and dreams of the future
My mind to a better place did it take

Tried to walk back to a place I knew
The freedom that is me
Happiness in silence
Laughter at all the simple things
Innocent like babies.

BREAKFAST WITH MUM

Heard the crack of a rifle
Walked through the glen of death
Screaming, blood and cramps down my leg
My world spiralling as I fell
I lay still, neck deep in mud
Mud trickles down with blood past me
Soldiers on foot pass me by
Trucks screeching to the pickup point
Thunderstorms and lightning
I await my company
My mind drifts to breakfast with mum
Scrambled eggs, bacon and pancakes
Close my eyes and pray for my rescue.

MOMENTS OF SILENCE

Close my eyes
A time to feel
My mind at peace
A time to find myself
My body at rest
A time to redirect my thoughts
Inhaling, breathe in the fresh air.

MORNINGS PROMISES RELIEF

Thunderstorms and lightning
Words like knives on my back
Tears, a luxury I do not have

Tornadoes and crushing sea waves
Strange silence within but stormy outside
Patience and gratitude for change, I am new

Howling winds, black sky and hailstones
The past, thoughts of freedom, I desire
Negativity a distant past, I reflect

Outside the eye of the hurricanes
The future I do not see, it's out of my hands
Selflessness I should embrace

Seismic shift and earthquakes
Structure and form that is new
Deeper delve into my inner core

Volcanic eruption molten flowing magma
Thoughts of serenity and bliss
Sleep like babies, flowing dreams

Vast snow in depth and rain rushing into the downs
Alone unfamiliar environment and turmoil within
Strange, weird new beginnings never imagined
Morning promises relief.

THAT WAS THE JOURNEY

Finally gave up the living
Eyes to the sky blank gaze, I'm not living
Shallow breath welcome relief
Clammy cold skin, feel my spirit lifting
My blood turns purple slow to move
Letting out the heat, perspiration
Hoarse voice those are my last words
My body ceases to tremble
Welcome relief
Tears roll down the corner of my eyes
My life pictured
I am back to my childhood
Full circle, that was the journey
Introversion, I can feel myself.

POEMS OF REFLECTION

DAYS OF LOVE

I loved my existence before
Days free of worry and toils
Sunlight in my face
Peace in my times

I loved my existence before
Days full of love and wonder
Silence that was peace
Life it was bliss

I loved my existence before
Days of dance and laughter
Sleep comes easy
Serenity all around

I loved my existence before
Days of pleasure and relaxation
Sweet love and sunny days
Love was all I had.

REFLECTION

I see a vision of me that's anger
A cold knife, my words cut through
I see freedom I desire, it hurts
Life crying out uncontrollable anger.

I see serenity a picture of peace, I desire
Stability indeed, it would be bliss
I see learning to forgive the way to humanity
Love fulfilled, I desire

I see life so fragile over anger
Unforeseeable circumstance over hurt
I see complete the who I am
Unimaginable force overpowers anger

I see spring morning sky so clear, what bliss
Orchestra the music of love
I see me, oh my, love nature's bliss
To have humanity the strength to learn to love.

TUSCAN ROSE

Had I known what grief would come
That has left me feeling numb

If I had known the choice I took
I should have taken another look

If I had taken another road
This life would not be a heavy load

If I had chosen peace
Her liberty release

If I had known this story had pain and sorrow
I would have looked out for my tomorrow

If I had known what love she needed
I would have submitted and headed

If I had known that's all it required
Love that was all encompassing and layered

If I had known, a love that was minimal, never
But to endure all things and endeavour

If I had known, it was a constant love under all weathers
I would have been a man and we would always be
together.

NO FLAWS

I want to know I lived this life
The best of me
Know I spent each hour and second knowing where I
was headed
Having no regrets
Express myself with no fear
Be in myself each day
Being honest and true to self
Stronger within me
Society can pass me by
I blend, knitted in its fabric
Know if I die today
Know who I was, in spite of what others saw
No flows in my character
My journey light, no spirit I carry
Make all my wrongs right
I see God and smile
I am a child in your eyes.

THE TRUTH

To tell the truth and not doubt yourself
To state what's on your mind and know honesty lives
Love with no regret and know it is all you have

To be true to yourself and know these are the days you
are living
To be good to others and know loyalty is abounding
Forgive and know that love exists

To be clear in your vision of the world and your place in
it
To be wise to earth and know you are on the right
direction.
This is your destiny, this is your truth.

SERENITY

A child's innocence
Eyes to see
Vision with no obscurity
Acceptance of your ways and all thy purity
Clear mind to reflect
Peace to rest at night
Glorious days to reflect on your wisdom
Hear the childlike voice that's my own
Those little things that I may miss and receive
Awareness of the human I am and love I should give
Openness of my mind to learn and see your ways
With you, full of laughter and joy, those are my days.

NO TEARS FOR ME

No tears for me
The depths of grief I cannot comprehend

Silent tears with no comfort
Free from torment, my body released

Talk till my last breath
The heart free from the world

Earth it departs, no baggage to carry
But the light, that has carried me

Spirit with joy lifts high
Lessons of life revealed

This my child is why you suffered
Why, it was so simple

Your destiny and time
Nothing else to gain but love

No wisdom, no love, no knowledge
I await my turn

The spirit flies
Freedom at last

No tears for me.

THE SEASONS

In my heart you always remain
Loyal and honest, you are my friend
From childhood, pictures and memories are everlasting
Journeys apart life's roads did take us
Maturity and experience and the road one travels
The seasons not this friendship changeth
My energy I would give
My time I would journey
In laughter and in sorrow union bonded stay forever.

THROUGH THE LOOKING GLASS

View the looking glass the face that belongs to me
To renew myself and not disdain the change
Turn back the seasons, happiness I seek and will find

Desire for the unborn child
Time has been unkind
Through the looking glass, hold back the time I was born

As life spans itself and the journey unfolds
Depart this life now and all will be meaningless
Counted by others as failure already

The story shall tell where success and failure will rest
As of now this life I must survive
In this life I must strive.

THE LIGHT IN THE WINDOW DIMMED

I woke up and the face of me I do not know
Feel like I am living in another dimension
Alien sensations, world I see and a world never dreamt
All of us are not like this, my life

No-one understands what I see
Everything strange I feel in me
Understood I cannot be, how was everything not me?
Me, I see not, voices I hear
Strange, I feel, I see everyone and wonder

There is a face they do not recognise
There is a voice they do not know
There is an accent they say is from far away
There is a different me every day

I tried to explain, I cannot
The world I know is unexplainable
The me I see I don't feel
My senses I do not feel
My dreams I do not feel
My humanity taken
The me I know is gone

How are you now?
I will tell you, no-one can comprehend
There's an end and certainty

There's a hardness that crumbles
This life is not what it's supposed to be
It's a little space
The space is not what everyone has
Freedom is not, what freedom is
I used to feel it in my core

To no end
Lose all humanity to meaninglessness
Waste time to meaninglessness
What did you gain in meaninglessness?
To everything there was me
That life felt unattainable and hard
Strange, heavy contrary was my world
Revealed a ruthless underworld I never envisaged
How did I get here?

UNHAPPY

All I could to make you happy
All I could I gave you plenty
All I could since I was twenty
All I could time now decays
And still you are not happy.

THIS LIFE YOU LIVE

A path no-one else follows
Experiences one alone understands
The road only you can travel
A road of maturity and growth
No tomorrow is promised
Plans are for the future
Positions, responsibilities and births
Blended and knitted into societies fabric
Find a place of your own
A corner of the world
That's the life one lives.

BLANK PAGE

A goodbye with no words
Words that are too painful to utter
Time wasted and life unfulfilled
Do not look back, the future beholds
Start again from the day of departure
Blank page, new life and new experiences
Find love in all the right places
A home to last. My soul at rest
Blended and knitted into the fabric of society
Happy memories are all that I carry
No more happy tears, false laughter and hateful words
A goodbye with no words
I never felt more at peace.

POEMS ON WISDOM

MY SOUL

When my soul leaves Earth do not cry for me
I am in the wind that whispers in the night
I am in the sun's rays that is the sunlight
I am in the silent stars that is the starlight
I am in the summer rain that cools the daylight
I am in the sea waves that hit the shores at night
That is how you know, I am always with you.

LIFE'S JUNCTION

There a is a point of knowledge
A knowledge and acceptance
Seismic shift, a parting of the ways
Indifference to the outcome of the situation
Life and time wasted

There is an understanding
A knowledge and acceptance
Life familiarity no more
Peace and understanding that was meant
The journey ends unlike it began

There is a junction in life
A knowledge and acceptance
Where the shadows of cruelty fall
Light's acceptance of departure
No golden sunrise our eyes shall meet
Empty skies and wounded hearts fly

There is no consolation
But a knowledge and acceptance
Even the light of day
The beauty that is the sea
Could return emotions of this life
Like a train out of the station, no returning here ever.

INNOCENCE NOT FOR THE WORLD

Innocence was lost
Protected mind and an unwanted child
Future unforeseen, I could have loved
Immature in my road, inexperienced in youth
Realisation of self
Life's struggle always
Learnt knowledge, suffering and tears
Hold on to the world
The world is not for the innocent
Save your soul for happiness
Suffer heaven heritage
Life is not a luxury.

LOSE MY POWER

Easy to love, easy to love
Not good at love
Everything I give
Trust comes easy
My heart is always open
Love wider than the Grand Canyon
Lose my power, my senses, my being
Spirit transferred
Led by love into the unknown
Heartbreak that's where it resides
Heartbreak I am aware
Man the hunter not satisfied
Never give in all or all you lose
Never settle or be stable
Emotions unavailable
The stranger friendly turned
Enemy mine
The love I thought we had
The love I thought we had.

EGO

Ego is part of a foolish man
Everything has a way of falling apart
Always be humble they say
Ego is unkind to the soul
Failure is certainly assured.

CHASING TIME

Clock hand, what matters
In the land, days and nights
Reverse years and months

Man and time, arrives and departs
The change of seasons
Just like sunlights and moonlights

Together comes all things
Perspective in lives
Just like rain and thunderstorms

Everything resembles the universe, summers and winters
The change of seasons
Time defines moments.

WHAT IF

What if I had trusted instinct? No tangent I would have taken
What if I had stayed, life's course, would my journey have been complete?

What if I had loved, my existence, would it have been different?
What if I had prayed, would the blessings enlighten my days?

What if I had smiled, would you have thought me less than who I am?
What if I had laughed, joy and energy to others, would you have known me well?

What if I had touched you, would you have changed your mind?
What if I had cried, would the world show me sympathy?

What if I had no hate, would karma pass me by?
What if I had never met you, would you have known who I was?

I WISH FOR YOU

I wish for you happiness in all you do
Love that is honest and true
Success and love of what you do
Strength and courage just like the man you are
Blessings upon blessings to fill your life with goodness
Laughter every day that is the medicine to happiness
Wisdom of the mind to direct your path
That is my wish for you.

UNUSUAL YOU

You that do not fit in, you that never wins
To the left is the right direction for you
You, that do not remember you
To you, everything is discovery, something new to the
eyes
You, who do not know where your fate lies
You, that is blessed with everything
To have everything but have nothing
You that others do not comprehend
To others, you are without wisdom and self-absorbed
To you, everything is just as it should be
You that was innocence gained knowledge
To you, everything in life happens in kind
You that do not know you, the one time left behind
To explain simply the miracle of heaven
You, that life seems too complex to attain
To you, others do not understand the human in you.

HAPPINESS

The silence, that is the night outside
The light, that is the stars above
The peace, that is in me without fear
The thoughts of tomorrow and what it brings

I am alone but happy
My sentience in my hands, I await direction
Me, feeling as I am supposed to be
A sense of something to come
Happiness when do you find it.